Amelia's
SCIENCE FAIR
DISASTER

by Marissa Moss

(except all experiments by Amelia)

Simon & Schuster Books for Young Readers

New York to Sydney

This notebook is dedicated to Golda Laurens
because I'd love to do a group project with her!

SIMON & SCHUSTER BOOKS FOR YOUNG READERS
An imprint of Simon & Schuster Children's Publishing Division
1230 Avenue of the Americas, New York, New York 10020
Copyright © 2008 by Marissa Moss

A Paula Wiseman Book

SIMON & SCHUSTER BOOKS FOR YOUNG READERS
is a trademark of Simon & Schuster, Inc.

Amelia® and the notebook design are
registered trademarks of Marissa Moss.

Book design by Amelia
(with help from Lucy Ruth Cummins)

← Good with any project!

Part of a fascinating scientific experiment! →

The text for this book is hand-lettered.
Manufactured in China

2 4 6 8 10 9 7 5 3 1

CIP data for this book is available from the
Library of Congress.

← where's the laboratory of Congress?

ISBN-13: 978-1-4169-6494-0
ISBN-10: 1-4169-6494-0

* first edition

If there are two words in the English language that DON'T go together, they're "science" and "fair." Sure, science can be fun, especially if you get to mix chemicals together and make explosions, but mostly it's serious business. Not because we're doing important experiments in science class, like figuring out how to cure cancer, but because one tiny mess-up can ruin EVERYTHING. It's kind of like baking (which is a type of chemistry, I guess), like the time my sister, Cleo, was making cookies and she ran out of flour so she used baking soda instead. GROSS!

Mom, taking a big bite out of Cleo's fresh-baked cookies.

YOU DID WHAT?

PTOOOIE!

Baking soda looks like flour. I didn't think it would make such a big difference.

I don't want to imagine what you'd use if you ran out of chocolate chips!

You have to be exact in science. Measure carefully, take notes, use only the right ingredients. A "fair" is something else entirely. That's where you go on rides, spend a lot of money to win cheap-o prizes, and eat too much fried everything.

fried pretzel

fried cookies

fried banana

fried cotton candy

fried pickle

fried oatmeal

There's even
fried ice cream!

So why do schools call it a "science fair" when they want kids to work really hard at some brilliant scientific idea and figure out how to explain it using cardboard and papier-maché? It's really a science contest (since you're judged – UGH!) or a science exhibit (since how good your display is matters as much if not more than the experiment itself).

main ingredients to any science fair

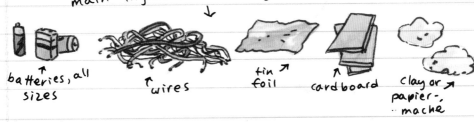

batteries, all
sizes

wires

tin
foil

cardboard

clay or
papier-
mache

I'd like an experiment that doesn't use ANY of these things, like : "Is there a food you _can't_ fry? What is it?"

If it was a <u>real</u> science fair, it would be like this:

Fun Rides

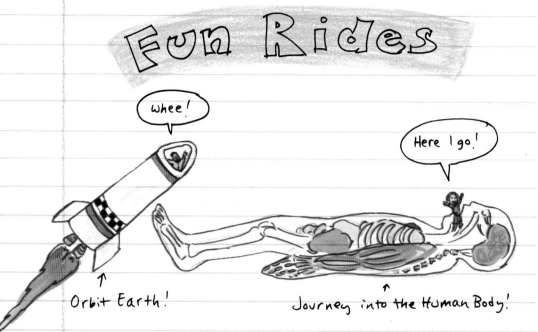

Orbit Earth!

Journey into the Human Body!

Shrink-O-Meter —
Become the Size of
an Atom!

Defy Gravity in the
Float-O-Chamber!

Junk Food

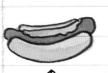

solar-cooked hot dogs

Invent-a-flavor Ice Slushes — here's botanical blue!

Fried atoms — you name it, we fry it!

Stupid Games

How cuddly!

Make an electrical circuit — win a giant stuffed battery!

Shoot your rocket the farthest — win a paper airplane!

Take me home to the cheese!

Oof — it's HEAVY!

Pick the smartest rat to finish the maze the fastest — win a rat!

Guess the density — win a balloon!

Of course, that's not what Mr. Engels, my science teacher, meant when he said we have to do a project for the school science fair. He didn't mean fun, games, and fried food. He meant work, work, and work.

Mr. Engels is a good teacher and mostly I like him, but he has tufts of hair coming out of the collar of his shirt. You can even see hair growing down his neck onto his back — UGGH! I'm so glad I'm not a boy when I see how hairy they can get! It's one step too close to looking like a rug.

Those are the other two words that should NEVER go together — Group Project. What that's supposed to mean is that two, three, or even four students work together, each contributing and doing their best to make a project that none of them could have done by themselves. They're supposed to appreciate each other's talents and blend them together into an amazing combination.

What it REALLY means is that one, maybe two, kids do most of the work and the others do a crummy job, so you end up with something WAY worse than what you could have done by yourself. PLUS you have the misery of nagging, begging, and fighting with the other kids, trying to get them to do their share.

Supposedly this experience is good social training. I think it's a form of torture or a bizarre social experiment for the teacher's entertainment.

So when Mr. Engels said to start thinking of a science fair group project it was DOUBLE misery — the four worst words together at once.

I wish Carly was in my class. Being with her is the only thing I can think of that could make it all bearable, even if we didn't end up in the same group. I know what she would say.

Come on, Amelia, have a sense of humor about it all!

Think of something really fun that you want to do and don't worry about the group project part.

That's what she'd say, but Carly hates group projects herself. There was the time she got stuck with two boys who just stared at her the whole time and were so nervous about talking to her, they couldn't do ANYTHING — it was pathetic! And that was one of her better groups.

Instead of thinking about a project, all I could think about was who my partners might be. It's slim pickings.

It wasn't exactly an inspiring group for a group project! The bell rang and it was time for lunch. I packed up my stuff and was heading for the cafeteria when the girl who asks a million questions — I think her name is Sadie — ran up to me.

Amelia, wait! What are you doing for the science fair? Do you have any ideas? I bet you do — you always do!

Do you look on the Internet?

Do you read books?

She didn't even wait for me to answer her questions, as if asking them was all that mattered — she didn't actually want any answers. She kept on talking and I kept on walking. It was ~~weird~~ ~~wierd~~ weird. ← I should do a project on finding a foolproof way to spell this stupid word!

She acted like we'd been friends forever — and I wasn't even sure what her name was! Finally I stopped walking and faced her. I had to do something to show her we weren't friends, that I barely knew her.

I have to admit, I was flattered to think ANYONE knew who I was. I'd never felt noticed before. It was nice. I mean that's not why I ran for student council — I did that for Carly because she wanted to be class president. Anyway, I thought all the attention would go to her because she was in the election debate and she's a cool person — I'm not — plus she's president. I'm only secretary.

But to hear Sadie talk you'd think I was just as cool as Carly. It felt good, but also strange, like I was wearing someone else's clothes, pretending to be somebody I wasn't. The way Sadie talked about me, I didn't recognize myself.

It started out feeling nice but the more she talked, the queasier I got. It was like Sadie had created some other person entirely in her imagination and stuck my face on that fantasy. Sure, some of the stuff she said was true, but the _way_ she said it made it into something else.

I didn't know what to say or do. I needed an excuse to get rid of her so when we passed a bathroom, I told her I'd see her later. But she said she needed to go too, so she followed me into the bathroom. I thought I'd go into a stall, then jump out real quick before she finished her business. Unfortunately it was the dreaded girl's bathroom in the 800 wing — the one that should NEVER, EVER be used.

evil toilet
↓

Hee, hee!

The toilet in the third stall always overflows, making the whole place SUPER GROSS. I was so eager to get rid of Sadie I didn't realize my mistake until I walked in and the stench gagged me.

I turned around and walked right out again, trying not to touch anything. Sadie followed me like a shadow.

"I thought you had to go," she said.

"I thought you did too!" I snapped.

?

!

It was a stand-off. I didn't want to admit I was just trying to lose her, and she didn't want to admit she was sticking to me, no matter what.

Why couldn't I simply tell her to go away? Why was I so worried about being nice and not hurting her feelings? She wasn't worried about not annoying me, or she'd have gotten the hint by now.

"I've got to go," I said. "I'm meeting a friend for lunch." There — that was a clear good-bye.

Not to Sadie. She took it as an invitation.

"You mean Carly? She's _too_ cool! Hey, can I eat lunch with you guys? That would be so great!"

I wanted to say no, I really did. But how could I do that without being rude? I was trapped!

"Okay," I mumbled. I guess I was hoping she wouldn't hear me clearly. Then I rushed off, trying to lose her in the throngs of students crowding the halls. But she was stickier than gum on my shoe — everywhere I turned, there she was.

I barrelled ahead with my face looking down and steam coming out of my ears. I was so mad at myself! Why did I say yes? Why was it so hard for me to say no? It's a short, simple word, easy to pronounce, so why was it almost impossible to say sometimes?

That made me think about all the times I'd said yes when I really meant no. It was turning into a bad habit — I had to get better at saying <u>NO</u>!

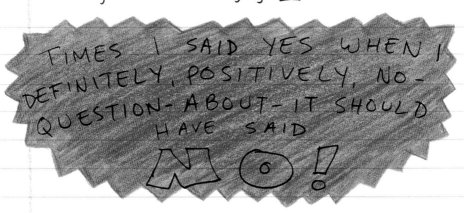

TIMES I SAID YES WHEN I DEFINITELY, POSITIVELY, NO-QUESTION-ABOUT-IT SHOULD HAVE SAID NO!

① When my dad asked me to go shopping with his wife, Clara, just the two of us so we could "bond" over clothes. As if!

Try this on! It'll look so cute on you!

frilly dress meant for a two-year-old

If I was a doll!

WAAH!

I'm telling my mom how mean you are to me!

I HATE YOU!

② When Mrs. Beloil asked me to babysit her bratty kid.

No amount of money is worth dealing with this big a brat!

And this was another time I DEFINITELY should have said **NO!** As soon as Sadie saw Carly, she ran up to her and gave her a hug like they were long-lost sisters.

Carly stared at me and mouthed "Who IS this?"

What could I say? This girl wasn't my friend. → she was more like a fan.

Finally Sadie let go. "Carly, you look gorgeous!"

"Do I know you?" Carly stepped back three paces.

"I'm Sadie, Amelia's friend." She said it like I'd won some big prize.

I shook my head. No, no, she's not — I barely know her. I hoped Carly could read what my eyes were trying to tell her.

Carly looked confused. I _had_ to say something.

"Really we just met. Sadie's in my science class."

Sadie elbowed me and giggled. "You're such a kidder! We got to know each other _last_ year — in Mr. L's class."

Was she joking? Or just plain crazy? I'd never even noticed her before! Maybe we were in the same class, but that hardly made us instant friends. We'd never had a conversation and here she was, acting like we were buddies from a long time ago.

I rolled my eyes.

I don't know this girl. We aren't friends... She's too much, too soon...

I wanted desperately for Carly to read my mind, for her to know that Sadie was making this all up.

Carly nodded. She acted like she believed Sadie! Then she turned to me and winked. What a relief! She understood! She knew Sadie was exaggerating times ten.

"I'm starving," Sadie said. "Let's go eat."

"I'm sorry," Carly lied, smooth as can be. "Amelia and I have a student council meeting. Byeee!" She hooked her arm in mine, waved at Sadie, and yanked me away. It was over in a minute— I was free!

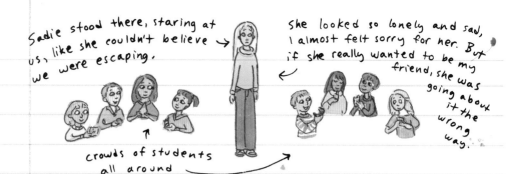

Sadie stood there, staring at us, like she couldn't believe we were escaping. →

← She looked so lonely and sad, I almost felt sorry for her. But if she really wanted to be my friend, she was going about it the wrong way.

crowds of students all around ⟶

"Carly, you saved my life! Thank you, thank you, thank you! I tried to get away from her, but I couldn't. You were brilliant!"

"It was easy, but really, Amelia, who IS that girl? She's like a crazy stalker. You've got to put up clear boundaries around someone like that. More than boundaries, you need thick, high walls."

Carly led us down a maze of corridors until we came to the corridor where the 6th graders ate lunch. What a genius idea! No one would look for a 7th grader anywhere near the place.

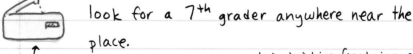

Certain wings, certain bathrooms, certain drinking fountains are totally off-limits if you don't want to be mistaken for a lowly 6th grader. I mean 6th grade isn't bad if you're in it, but once you move on, you need to stay moved on.

"I know," I said, sitting on a bench next to Carly and unwrapping my lunch. "And I tried. But she's so pushy and I didn't want to be rude or hurt her feelings."

"I mean," I went on, "she's not a bad person. She's just..." Actually, I wasn't sure what she was.

"Desperate?" Carly offered.

"Yeah, that's it — desperate." I bit into my sandwich. "At first I was kind of flattered because she liked me so much. Then it felt strange, off somehow, because she doesn't really _know_ me. It was like she wanted to be friends with an imaginary person who looked like me, but wasn't."

"I don't know about that. She's been watching you for over a year, so she probably thinks she knows you well by now."

I shuddered. "Ick — that's creepy!"

"No, it's sad," said Carly. "She really, REALLY wants to be your friend. That's what makes her so desperate."

I thought about that. What was wrong with Sadie wanting to be my friend so much? No one had ever chosen me like that. It was flattering. I couldn't help liking that she'd picked me out of everybody. Maybe we could be friends.

"Maybe it's not so sad," I said. "Is it that strange for someone to pick me as a friend?"

"Of course not! I picked you, didn't I?" Carly said.

"No, I picked you. I came to you. I just wasn't as pushy as Sadie." I thought about that — was I any different than Sadie? I'd noticed Carly right away, as soon as I saw her. She was so confident and smart and funny. I knew I wanted to be her friend. I knew I wanted to know her better.

I remember the first time I saw Carly. She was laughing with Maya. There was just something about her I liked. ↳

Then she was assigned to be my partner when we built rockets for science. And I saw she kept a notebook (like me) and loved science (like me). That's all it took — we became partners and friends at the same time. All because of a group project! That's NOT what was happening with Sadie, but it was an interesting coincidence that we had science together.

"Maybe Sadie is pushy, but she's just trying to be friends the way she knows best. What's wrong with that?" I asked.

"It's the way too buddy-buddy part that creeps me out. She acts like we're <u>already</u> best friends, not like she wants to <u>become</u> friends." Carly shook her head. "She's not normal."

Normal. That's a hard thing to be, especially in middle school. I mean, what IS normal? It's the thing everyone wants to be but no one is sure exactly how to do it, how to fit in and be "normal." Or there are people who don't want to be normal at all — they want to stand out from the crowd, to be exceptional (in a good way, of course). Carly, for example, is certainly not normal or typical or average. I hope I'm not either.

But I don't want to be "not normal" the way Carly says Sadie is. That's the bad kind of not being normal, the kind that's the kiss of death in middle school.

Sometimes it feels like you have to walk a tightrope in order to fit in yet not be boring.

↓

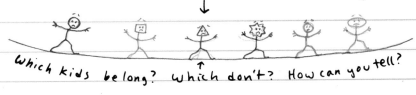

Which kids belong? Which don't? How can you tell?

CHART of NORMALNESS

STRANGE	NORMAL	EXCEPTIONAL

IN CLOTHING

overalls, jumpers, long skirts — the kind of clothes <u>no one</u> wears anymore

jeans, T-shirts, regular shirts, nothing noteworthy

stylish things like bow ties, vests, hats, suspenders

IN HOBBIES

The pink ones are the juiciest!

collecting bottle caps, chewing rubber bands, knitting sweaters for aliens

Playing soccer, skateboarding, Playing guitar or piano

winning Olympic medals, sky diving, creating sculptures

IN SCIENCE PROJECTS

proving catsup is a vegetable, dissecting aliens, carving mt. Rushmore on a bar of soap

baking soda volcanoes, plants, models of the universe

DNA testing, building a motor, curing cancer

Luckily Sadie wasn't in the rest of my classes, only science, so I didn't have to think about where she fit on the normalness chart. Unluckily, Mr. Engels assigned our groups the next day. Out of all the kids in the class, he put me with the two I <u>least</u> wanted — Sadie and Felix, the boy who sleeps through class. How much work could I expect from him? It was like Sadie was my only partner, with no buffer of another person.

We had to meet in our groups and brainstorm ideas.

drool ↗
coming
out of his mouth

I'm so, SO, SO excited we're doing this together!

It's going to be so FUN!!

There was no room for any of my ideas. I felt like I could fall asleep next to Felix and Sadie would go on yakking.

So, what ideas do you have? I have TONS of ideas. First of all, we're going to pretend that Felix here doesn't exist. He's hopeless. I had to do a project with him once in social studies and I couldn't get him to talk to me. I ended up doing EVERYTHING and signing his name on it. So forget about him. There's LOTS of stuff we could do...

↑ I wondered if Felix had tried to talk to her and she didn't hear because she was so busy gabbing.

I could tell this group would be a disaster. I asked Mr. Engels if I could please, please, PLEASE change groups. He said no. "You're a smart girl, Amelia, I'm sure you'll figure out how to work with your group."

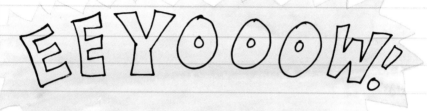

EEYOOOW!

I wanted to scream! It was obvious what I'd figure out — the golden rule that anyone who's done a group project knows: Those who work hard have to work extra hard to make up for those who don't work, work badly, or hardly work. Group projects don't make you appreciate people's "special" contributions. They make you resent having to do more work so that all of you can get a decent grade.

Maybe I'm wrong. Maybe group projects can be fair, but it's never been that way for me.

← Except for ONCE — that rocket project with Carly. Then it was just her and me and we both cared about our grade and what each other thought.

GROUP PROJECTS I'VE DONE AND DESPISED

The model of the California mission made out of styrofoam-carving it was like trying to cut paper dolls out of a rubber bathmat!

It looked like an earthquake-the Big One-had already demolished it.

We couldn't put the roof on because the walls were so uneven.

The report on Martin Luther King Jr.

One kid was in charge of his childhood. She wrote three sloppy sentences and that was it.

Another kid was supposed to write about protests and demonstrations. He printed out pages from the Internet and thought that was good enough.

I had to write about his speeches, especially the most famous "I have a dream" one and I added drawings and quotes from other people about their reactions. I worked really hard - and, thanks to my partners, got a C.

The ancient Egyptian pyramid →

It ended up looking like a pile of dog poo. It stank!

Not to mention the botched report on the American Revolution and the hideous diorama of a tropical rain forest — all projects I spent a LOT of time on only to get crummy grades because of my partners. I didn't want that to happen this time.

I knew Felix wouldn't contribute anything except drool and snores. But what about Sadie, my instant best friend? How could I work with someone who was so enthusiastic and super sweet? Maybe that would be a good thing — it would make up for Felix's blobbiness. Sadie would definitely work hard. I just had to survive her constant yakking and high pitch of excitement — that and the fact that now she REALLY would think we're best friends.

It was overwhelming. Sadie had too many ideas and she wasn't good at listening to anyone else.

I had to wave her down to shut her up.
↓

Hold it a minute! You're talking too much and too fast.

Why don't we each think of three projects and tomorrow we'll pick one.

"Only three?" Sadie squealed.

"It'll be easier that way," I said. Felix didn't say anything. I wondered if he'd wake up to help pick which project. Probably not and then it would be my choice against Sadie's. I decided to worry about that later. For now I was relieved I'd managed to _say_ something.

I thought I'd have to race out of class to avoid getting stuck with Sadie for lunch, but lucky for me, Mr. Engels asked her to stay after and help him sort through boxes of equipment for possible projects.

wires and electrical stuff
↳

test tubes and beakers
↓

cogs, gears, wheels
↓

↗
Sadie leaped at the opportunity. She promised to snag anything cool for us to use — even though we have NO idea what we're doing yet.

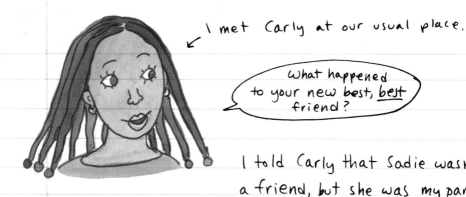

I met Carly at our usual place.

What happened to your new best, _best_ friend?

I told Carly that Sadie wasn't a friend, but she _was_ my partner for the science fair. Carly nearly choked on her banana.

"You're kidding, right? Of all the kids in the class, what are the odds you'd be stuck with her? This is going to be interesting!"

"What do you mean?" I asked. I had a feeling it wasn't something good.

"Well, now you _have_ to be her friend — or at least act friendly. How can you make a good project if you're enemies?"

"Are those the only choices — friends or enemies? Can't we just be partners, people doing a job together?"

Carly shook her head. "Not if she insists on being your friend, which she does."

I sighed. "Okay, we'll be friends until we finish the project. Then I'll say I'm too busy to be her friend."

Carly rolled her eyes. "Like that will work!"

"What else can I do?" I felt trapped.

"You could be honest. Tell her she's not your type."

I remembered Elana from second grade. I really liked her, though now I can't say why. →

I tried to sit near her at lunch and I invited her to my birthday party (but she didn't come). I was too shy to actually talk to her. I just hoped she'd notice me. She never did. Or maybe I wasn't her type.

I had to give Sadie some credit. At least she had the guts to tell me she liked me. I didn't want to be honest if it meant hurting her feelings. Whether I wanted to be her friend or not, I owed her that consideration. Anyway, she had to know that you can't <u>make</u> someone be your friend. It's a mysterious chemical reaction that just happens — or doesn't.

That got me thinking about science. Maybe I could think of a project that showed how when you mix some things together, they combust while others do nothing. Why do some chemicals react to each other while others have no reaction at all?

Except the obvious example was the baking-soda-and-vinegar volcano — the last thing I wanted to do for our project.

I wondered why Carly and I were friends, why did we mix so well? Maybe some things can't be defined or measured — they just are. Not everything is a science. Some things are mysteries.

"So what are you doing for your project?" Carly asked.

"We haven't decided yet. Do you have any suggestions?"

"Not for you! I'm saving my ideas for my own group. I'm working on a project too, you know. And I've got a good group — Ezra and Letitia. They're both smart at science and as an extra bonus, they're nice."

Ezra is funny and loud and everyone → likes him.

I had French with him last year and he cracked up the class with ← his jokes.

Letitia is shy and smart and really generous. Carly told me she baked cookies for the whole science class once.

It was so unfair! Carly got <u>two</u> great partners! She was with kids you'd <u>want</u> to have as friends, kids you'd like to hang out with. I felt stuck in Loserville with snoring Felix and babbling Sadie.

I had a sinking feeling that was why Mr. Engels had put us together — we were the losers no one wanted in their groups.

I was a reject like Felix and Sadie — ouch, that hurt!

"Come on, Amelia, you're not a loser. It's true you have a crummy group, but that doesn't make you a crummy person. Besides, Sadie's not horrible. She's just exhausting to be around. She tries too hard."

I knew Carly was trying to make me feel better, but it wasn't working.

"Do you know anyone who likes Sadie? Maybe she's so eager to be my friend because no one else is loser enough to accept her." I tried to remember if I'd ever seen Sadie hang out with other kids but to be honest, I'd never noticed her — aside from nicknaming her the girl who asked a million questions — until she came up to me that day in science class.

I decided to change the subject. "Come on, tell me what your project is. You know I won't copy you."

"You better not!" Carly warned. "Anyway, we're not sure yet. Either how you _can_ make oil and water mix by adding a secret ingredient or how to separate hydrogen from oxygen in water."

They both sounded cool. I was impressed.

oil →

water dyed red so → you can easily see the distinct layers

Add the secret ingredient, shake it up...

...and presto change-o, it becomes one blended liquid! How?

"We're meeting at Ezra's after school today to decide on which project and who will do what."

I couldn't help it, I was jealous of Carly. That was exactly the way a group project was supposed to work, with everyone doing their share, no fighting, just a lot of shared energy. Why couldn't I have that?

HOW TO MAKE A GOOD, SUCCESSFUL GROUP PROJECT

DO'S!

① Do your share of the work. (You can't complain about others if you don't.)

② Do be appreciative of other people's work.

There! My model of the Statue of Liberty for our New York project is finished.

And it only looks a little like a hunchback.

Wow, your Brooklyn Bridge's wobbliness matches my statue!

← Oops! Glue spilled here.

③ Do try to be neat because sloppiness brings down everyone's grade.

It doesn't matter how well I follow the Do's and avoid the Don'ts — I have a feeling this will be a difficult group project. I was searching the Internet for ideas when Cleo bellowed outside my door.

Telephone! For you! Someone called Sadie!

↑ Hearing Cleo made me think we could do something on moose calls or rate sounds from annoying to unbearable, create a new decibel scale.

I was surprised that Sadie was calling me at home. Okay, we were partners. It was normal for her to look up my number and use it, but Carly was right — I needed boundaries, big, thick walls. I glared at Cleo and took the phone.

Can't we talk at school? I'm busy — I can't talk now.

Even when I said I had to go, Sadie kept on talking, telling me all the great ideas she had for projects. Finally I put down the phone and went back to the computer.

When I picked up the receiver ten minutes later, she was still yakking away. She hadn't even noticed I wasn't there!

That was it — enough was enough! "Look, Sadie, I REALLY have to go," I interrupted her. "Byeee!" She was probably still talking, but I'd hung up.

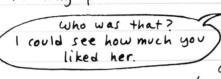

Who was that? I could see how much you liked her.

Cleo leaned in the doorway of my room, waiting to take back the phone.

"She's my partner for the science fair, and you're right — I don't like her. But I'm stuck with her. Unfortunately she really likes me."

"Wow," said Cleo, "That's a new one — someone who likes you, but you don't like them rather than the other way around. If I were you, I'd enjoy it. It'll never happen again."

"Thanks a lot, Cleo!" I snapped.

"Come on, Amelia, admit it. Isn't it nice to have someone want to be your friend? To have someone think you're cool?"

As soon as Cleo said it, I knew she was right. Sadie thought I was cool. Even Carly didn't think that. Did I really want to throw that away? Couldn't I make some sort of friendship with Sadie work? I could try.

I could start by doing whatever project she wanted to do. That would mean for once I'd do less work on a group project because I would skip the whole beginning research stage. But it would also mean working on something that wasn't my idea. It was a tough choice,

Well, not that tough. Sadie had so many ideas, chances were good I'd be happy with one of them. So for my three ideas to bring to class tomorrow I wrote down:

① whatever
② Sadie
③ wants

I love it when homework is that easy!

Since my science was done, I moved on to math, a subject where there are never any group projects — or projects at all!

↓

Mr. Engels had us meet in our groups again today, but he said this is our last chance to use class time. From now on we're supposed to work together at home.

our cozy little group got together with Felix in his usual place, snoring between us.

Should we TRY to include Felix?

Or just put his name on the project when we're done?

ZZZZZZ

Maybe we could include him as part of our experiment — like what kind of alarm works best to wake someone up?

I meant it as a joke (a not-so-funny, annoyed one), but Sadie thought it was a great idea. Plus we'd get Felix to participate doing exactly what he does best — sleeping. After all, group projects are about appreciating everyone's talents.

So even though I'd decided not to suggest any ideas for projects and to go along with whatever Sadie came up with, the Sleeping Felix became our science fair project.

We wrote up a summary like this:

The scientific question: Which works better at waking people up, a LOUD sound or an ANNOYING sound?

Materials needed: a sleeping person, a recording of four loud sounds, a recording of four annoying sounds.

Procedure: Collect all sounds on a CD. Play each sound before sleeping person. Observe which sounds wake him up. Record observation and draw a conclusion.

Conclusion: To be made after sounds are played and the scientific question is answered.

For coming up with an experiment in twenty minutes, I thought we'd done pretty good. Maybe we could work well as a group after all. Felix did his part and slept, Sadie offered to find the loud sounds, and I'm going to find the irritating ones. As soon as we do all the recording, we'll do a trial with Felix and write down our observations and conclusion.

I never thought a partner who slept all the time could be a good thing. →

But Felix was truly useful - he was a key part of our experiment. We couldn't do it ← without him.

I was in such a good mood, I did the unthinkable —
I invited Sadie to eat lunch with me and Carly.

Really?
you mean it?

Great!
I mean really
great, really,
truly GREAT!

She was so happy about it, it was embarrassing.
I couldn't imagine ANYONE caring that much about
eating their sandwich next to me. I wondered if she
was just desperate for any friend. Maybe it wasn't
me she was interested in, but anyone who was
alive and eating lunch.

The worst thing in middle school is eating by yourself. If that
was what Sadie normally did, no wonder she was so grateful.

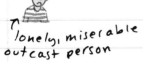

lonely, miserable
outcast person

everyone else, happy, talking, busy with
friends, clearly not rejects

Carly didn't seem surprised when she saw me with
Sadie. But she wasn't very friendly, so I had to be
super nice to make up for her rudeness. When Sadie
went to throw away her trash, I let Carly have it.

"Why are you being so cold to Sadie? You're not exactly welcoming!"

Why should I be? Did you ask _me_ if I minded Sadie joining us? Did _I_ have a choice in this? I don't have to be her friend just because you decided to be hers. And why did you, anyway? Get some backbone, Amelia, and be honest.

You don't like her — you just don't have the guts to tell her.

You mean I'm not nasty enough to tell her. Look, she's my science partner. We have to be able to work together.

Being partners doesn't make you instant friends.

I'm not her friend. I'm just friendly. There's a difference.

Oh, yeah? Explain that to _her_!

Carly and I both froze when Sadie bounced back toward us, like an overeager puppy. She was practically wagging her tail, she was so happy to be part of our group.

But I wasn't happy. I felt like a liar. Carly was right — I wasn't being honest. But what's more important, telling the truth or not hurting someone's feelings?

Carly glared at me and stalked off. I had Sadie all to myself for the rest of lunch. I didn't mean to trade my best friend for a girl I didn't even like, but it looked like that was what I'd done.

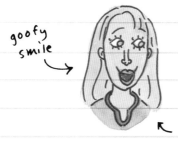

goofy smile →

Sadie was totally unaware of any problem. She just chattered on and on about the most boring things possible, describing plots of TV shows and lists of clothes in her closet. No wonder she didn't have any friends!

Except me, her fake, not really, no way → friend. Or friend only until our project was done. I gritted my teeth and told myself I only had to put up with her until the science fair. Then I'd never have to talk to her again.

My cheeks felt stiff from smiling and forcing myself to say nothing.

Usually I walk home with Carly after school, but she wasn't waiting for me in our regular place. That was a sign she was still mad at me.

So I walked home by myself.

Until I heard footsteps running behind me. It was Sadie.

"I thought we could work on the science project at your house today," she said. First she called me without me giving her my phone number. Now she was inviting herself over,

"There's no more class time," Sadie said, "so we have to work at home."

"But not at MY house!" I snapped. I'd tried so hard not to be rude to Sadie, but Carly was right — the nicer I was, the pushier she got. After all, we could each work at our own homes — apart from each other.

"Don't be such a grouch! We can go to my house if you want. I'm just trying to do what's best for the project. And our grade."

I didn't want to go to Sadie's house, either. I just wanted to be left alone. But she was right — we had to get the project done and it would be quicker and easier if we worked together.

"Fine," I said. "We'll work at my house. But let's finish everything today or at least enough so that we can do the rest by ourselves, then meet at school to put our parts together. I don't want to do this at home again." I meant I didn't want to have her over again. I hoped she got the message.

It felt like Sadie → was a stray dog, following me home and eager to be adopted.

But I wasn't feeling very warm or welcoming. ← I wanted to growl, "Back off!"

It took us over an hour to sort through different sounds and agree on our top picks. We were finishing the list at the kitchen table when Cleo came in for a snack.

Who's your little friend, Amelia?

Did Carly finally dump you? I knew it was just a matter of time.

The only thing worse than having Sadie at my house was Cleo seeing Sadie there. Or maybe it was Sadie seeing Cleo. Both were bad.

"Go away, Cleo. We're working," I said.

"I have the right to eat. I live here, you know." She ignored me, sticking her jelly-roll nose into the refrigerator, then into the cupboard, then back into the refrigerator.

"So what are you guys working on so hard?" she asked, chewing a hunk of salami.

"Annoying sounds — and you're the most annoying of all!"

Sadie giggled, which was the next most annoying sound. I was surrounded by irritating noises!

typical Cleo snack — plate piled high with crackers, cheese, olives, and carrots

Cleo dug around the kitchen, put together a huge snack, and flounced out. Sadie watched her every move.

"Your sister's hilarious! I like her!" she said.

Another mark against Sadie.

"She could be useful at least," I said. "I could record her eating, chewing gum, snoring, or singing. Any of those would be a great annoying sound for our experiment."

Sadie giggled again. I had to dig my nails into my palms to keep from yelling at her. She was almost as annoying as Cleo!

She looked all sweet and innocent, but Carly was right — she was hard to be around. →

The real science experiment would be whether I could be polite and finish the project or would I end up screaming at Sadie and ruin everything. ←

I tried to set clear boundaries like Carly said. Yes, Sadie was in my house, but I deliberately on purpose did NOT bring her into my room. I made sure we worked in the kitchen even though Cleo could interrupt us that way. Because being in my room would let Sadie know more about me and she'd _really_ think she was my friend.

It was bad enough she'd met Cleo. At least Mom was still at work. I didn't want her to know anything more about my life. She was my partner and we had to work together, but that was it!

Of course Sadie asked if she could see my room. I said it was too messy and the kitchen was more comfortable. But when I went to the bathroom and came back, Sadie was gone.

I had a BAD feeling about where she was. Sure enough, my door was open. I knew I'd left it shut — I always do.

And there she was. She'd invaded my room and even worse SHE WAS READING

MY NOTEBOOK!!!!

I yanked the book out of her hand and pulled her from the room. →

I was yelling so loud, I could have been a sound for our experiment. I was FURIOUS!

Luckily this was a new notebook and I hadn't written much in it — and nothing about Sadie.

GET OUT

I DON'T EVER WANT TO SEE YOU AGAIN!

She started babbling lame excuses, "I'm sorry. I didn't realize it was private. I was just curious. I'm SO sorry!"

I was so mad, I was shaking. I heard the front door shut and I knew she'd left.

Cleo came running into my room. "What happened? What's all the yelling about?"

"She snooped — in my room and IN MY NOTEBOOK! I HATE HER!!!"

Cleo looked surprised. "That's awful! What a jerk!"

I couldn't help it — I started to cry. "I tried so hard _not_ to be rude to her, to be a good partner, and look what it got me. Carly was right. Sometimes you have to be rude. It's better to tell the truth than be nice and lie."

Usually Cleo's pretty bratty, but she wasn't then. She really got it.

You don't have to be rude to be firm, but Carly's right — you need to be straight with people. You can't be fake with them.

I should have been absolutely clear I didn't want to be her friend. Why did I care more about her feelings than my own? Why did I try to be "the nice girl"?

Everyone tells us to be nice, but that's not always right.

I couldn't help smiling. Cleo's the most not-nice person I know. She has NO problem being rude or saying no or being clear about what she wants. Strange to think I should admire Cleo, but those are qualities I really want to have.

But what about the science project? I still had Sadie for a partner, a partner I didn't trust AT ALL.

"Here's what I would do," Cleo suggested. "Do your part, write it up, and let Sadie take care of her own stuff. So what if she doesn't do a good job. So what if your grade is lower because of her. That's the way it is with group projects." Cleo shrugged. "The most important thing is to admit that you can't control other people. You can't make them work the way you want them to. Sometimes you'll get a good group. Sometimes you won't. Myself,

Maybe I can work on saying no and not → being fakey nice, but I don't want to be a bad group person.

I try to be the problem person in the group. Then maybe no one else will be. But you're not like that."

She was right — I'm not.

That's not for me, though I see how it fits Cleo.

Could I change? Could I be the partner who did no work for once? Could I NOT care about grades? I liked the idea that Sadie would get a bad grade all because of me, but could I really do that?

That night I had a terrible nightmare. I was at the science fair looking at all the projects.

the predictable volcano

the one with clear diagrams and pages and pages of data

the one with test tubes and beakers

the one with batteries, wires, and lightbulbs

the one with plants

the one that was a model of the universe

Some were neat. Some were sloppy. But one was worst of all. It looked (and smelled) like a pile of garbage.

Everyone was laughing at the mess. I went closer
to see whose project it was. And there it was - MY NAME!
It was MY project, my group's, that is.

I woke up sweating, my heart pounding. I couldn't
purposely do a bad job on the group project even if
it would hurt Sadie (and serve her right!) because
it would hurt me, too. I'd have to do what Cleo
said — just grit my teeth, do my best, and not care
about the rest of my group.

I lay awake thinking for a long time, but I couldn't figure
out a better solution.

↓

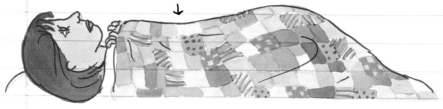

In the morning I decided to do what I usually did
when I had a hard problem and wasn't sure what
to do. I wrote to Nadia.

Even though I moved away, we're still good friends, and she still gives me great advice. ↘

Dear Nadia,
Remember when we had the group project on the water cycle in 3rd grade? You and I did all the work and Chelsea did almost nothing. It was so unfair — but at least we had each other to work with. This time there's NO ONE in my group I can depend on for the science fair project. One partner sleeps all the time. The other one is a fink. I don't want to help them out, I don't want to do everything. But I don't want to fail either. What would you do? Yours till the slide shows,
amelia

Nadia Kurz
61 South St.
Barton, CA
91010

I always felt better after writing to Nadia, as if now she had my problem, so I didn't have to think about it anymore.

I wanted to talk to Carly, too. I hoped she wasn't still mad at me. We both have French together first period so I went right up to her and told her about Sadie.

Amelia, I'm so sorry! I knew that girl was too pushy, but a snoop? I wouldn't have guessed that. She was too desperate for a friend, too needy for me to be comfortable around her, but I never would have suspected!

Is that what she was? Desperate? Needy? I'm not so sure. I think she was sneaky — she was plotting to read my notebook all along.

As soon as I said it, I realized how silly that sounded. Why would anyone plot to do that? But I felt so betrayed, that's what it seemed like even if it wasn't true.

Allez, les enfants! Attention!

Ouvrez votres livres à la page huit.

I was glad to be distracted by French verbs. Mr. Le Poivre interrupted us. And for once

By the time I had science, I was calm and collected. I'd decided exactly how I was going to act around Sadie — the frozen treatment. I would absolutely, completely ignore her.

I did. It drove her crazy.

icicles

Now Sadie was REALLY desperate! ↙

Please, Amelia, I'm so SO SO sorry! There's no excuse for what I did. I'm a terrible person. You must hate me. I know you don't want to be friends.

But we need to work together—please!

Hmmm, is that a fly buzzing around?

Pesky thing, isn't it?

I used that strategy for a week or so. Meanwhile I collected my annoying sounds and put them on a CD.

GNAAK

① a garbage disposal with a stone caught in it

EZZZZ

② a mosquito's whine

ZZZZZZZ

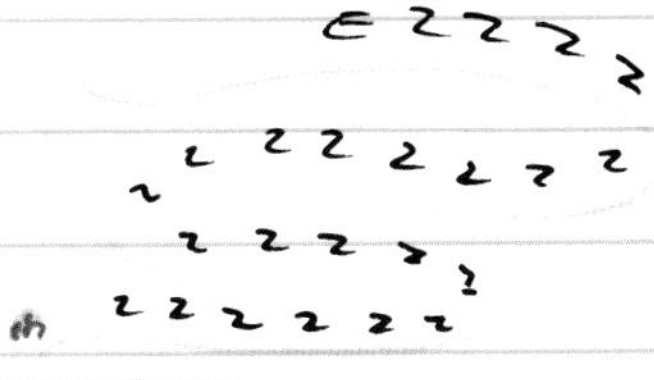

③ a crying baby

WAAAAH!

④ Cleo slurping soup

SHLOOOP

The problem was, I needed the other half of the experiment, the loud noises, in order to draw a conclusion. How could I tell which type of sound worked best on Felix if I only had one kind?

I was stuck. Either I had to talk to Sadie or I had to do _her_ work as well as mine. Which would be worse?

DIFFICULT CHOICES OR WEIGHTY DILEMMAS

These are the questions they should ask on standardized tests, but they don't. Too bad because these are the things you really need to know.

↓

① Which is worse - hurting your friend's feelings or getting in trouble with your mom?

② Which is worse — hurting your friend's feelings or getting in trouble with your sister?

③ Which is worse — sitting next to someone with heavy perfume or someone chewing gum loudly?

④ Which is worse — going to school or spending a day sick in bed?

Which was the worse of these two evils? It was a tough choice. I couldn't decide. So instead I gave myself one more day before I <u>had</u> to pick one over the other. Maybe a brainstorm would come to me while I was sleeping. Maybe Nadia would answer my postcard.

When I got home from school, there it was — my answer! A postcard from Nadia!

Dear Amelia,
You know me — I can't help it, I do the work no matter what. I admit I care a <u>LOT</u> about my grades. I <u>need</u> to get A's and I feel awful when I don't, so I'll do everyone's part to be sure of a good grade. That's why I <u>hate</u> group projects! I wish I could accept a C, but I can't — I just can't. But that's <u>my</u> problem. Yours till the pen tips,
Nadia

NON-EDIBLE FOODS

LIVER 8¢

Famous Race Horses "The Old Grey Mare" 294

Amelia
564 N. Homerest
Oopa, Oregon
97881

I cared about grades too, but not like Nadia.
I thought about my science fair nightmare. I
didn't want everyone to think my project was
garbage, but it didn't have to get an A either.

That night at dinner Cleo asked how the
project was going. I said it was halfway done
and I couldn't do any more.

"Can't or won't?" she asked.

I sighed. "Won't, I guess."

"Amelia!" Mom said. "That's not like you! You
should do your best work!"

I didn't want to explain the whole ugly mess to
Mom, so I excused myself and went to call Carly.

When I was done, she said, "You know what
you have to do, so do it."

"But I don't know! That's the problem!" I protested.

"Yes," Carly was firm. "You do. You know exactly what to do. See ya tomorrow." And she hung up.

How could she be so sure? I wasn't sure, not at all. But then I realized she was right. I did know what to do. I'd known all along. I didn't _want_ to do it, but I knew it was the right thing, at least for me.

So I picked up the phone and made another call. To Sadie.

I wasn't mean or angry or friendly or chatty. I was pure business. I told her what I needed her to bring to school tomorrow, I told her how the experiment would work. I told her how we'd write it all up and present it on a big piece of cardboard.

When I hung up the phone I felt, I don't know — I felt capable. Like I could face an unpleasant task and do it well. It felt like a grown-up thing to do, a grown-up way to act.

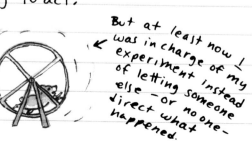

maybe we're all like hamsters on a wheel, all part of a giant experiment on how to grow up. It's tricky.

But at least now I was in charge of my experiment instead of letting someone else — or no one — direct what happened.

The next day in French, Carly didn't say anything about Sadie. Instead she talked about her own science project.

"We've made it interactive, not just something you look at or read. It's not complicated science, but I think our display is so good, we could win a prize."

"I can't wait to see it," I lied. I wasn't going to fail. I'd end up with a presentation, but I knew Carly's group would do a WAY better job. I didn't need her to remind me how much better you can do when you have a good group — you can even have fun.

"Do you want to go together?" Carly asked.

"Go where? To what?" I'd stopped paying attention to what Carly was saying because I didn't need any more reminders of how wonderful my project was <u>wasn't</u>.

Carly raised an eyebrow. →

Were you listening at all?

To the science fair this Saturday. We have to go early to set up in the gym. Do you want to go together? Answer now — this is a limited offer.

"I guess so." I realized this was another time when I wanted to say no, but didn't. I didn't want to admit to Carly that I was jealous of her and her group, and I didn't want to seem petty. So even though I didn't want to watch her and her friendly, helpful, hard-working group set up their amazing, fun, creative project, I said yes.

On the way to science, I tried to make my face look firm and serious. When I saw Sadie, she looked scared and I almost felt sorry for her. Then I remembered her snooping in my notebook and I felt hard and tough.

"Here," she mumbled, putting a CD on my desk. "Those are my loud sounds. We can test them on Felix after class."

I explained to Mr. Engels what we wanted to do and he agreed. He looked like he was trying not to laugh.

zz zzzzzzz

I guess it was a funny experiment. →

when the bell rang and everyone rushed out for lunch, he was still there, his cheek wet with drool.

Felix slept through everything, as usual.

We put Sadie's CD in the class computer and played the first sound, a jackhammer. Felix didn't blink. Then came the second sound, cymbals crashing with a ringing echo. I covered my ears, but he didn't flinch. The third sound was the roar of a jet engine. The fourth was an explosion. Felix slept through them all.

Next we tried my CD. Felix didn't budge through the garbage disposal, the whining mosquito, or the crying baby. He did twitch when Cleo slurped the soup. But he didn't wake up, not for any of it.

It was a disaster! Our experiment was a total failure. Neither kind of sound was more effective.

"What do we do?" I asked Mr. Engels. "Our experiment didn't work."

"Then that's what you conclude," he said. "Experiments often don't turn out the way we expect. That's science."

Mr. Engels got out his lunch, took a bag of chips and started to open it.

It made a crisp shuuff sound.

Felix sat bolt upright, wide awake.

Lunch? It's time for lunch?

I'd never seen him with his eyes open before.

I thought he'd sleep through the rest of school.

He grabbed his backpack... →

...and dashed out of the room - he was actually fast!

I stared at Mr. Engels. "Did you know that would happen?"

"How do you think I get him out of here every day?" He chuckled.

I grinned. "So that's the solution to our experiment — it's not loud or irritating noises that wake up Felix. It's food noises! And good ones, like chip bags opening. Not bad ones like Cleo slurping." I turned to Sadie. "I'll draw up the irritating noises. You do the loud ones. And I'll do the conclusion."

"No," Sadie begged. "Let me do it. Please!"

This was another time I wanted to say no. I wanted to be sure our presentation was the best possible and that meant me doing it. And it would've been easy for once to say no.

But when I opened my mouth, I said, "Okay - you do it."

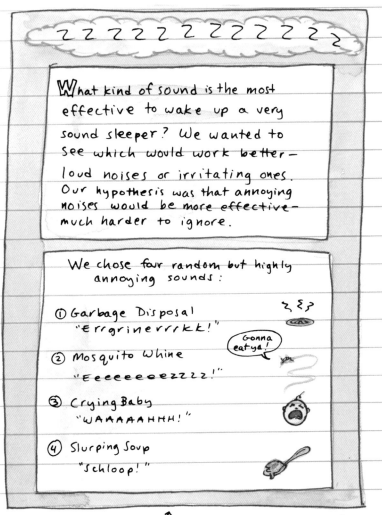

I had absolutely no reason to trust Sadie. And there I was, doing just that. There was no scientific explanation for it, just as there isn't for so many things in life, especially in middle school.

proof there's life on mars ↑

That night I wrote up the introduction, explained the experiment, then drew pictures of my irritating sounds. When I was done, it looked like this:

What kind of sound is the most effective to wake up a very sound sleeper? We wanted to see which would work better— loud noises or irritating ones. Our hypothesis was that annoying noises would be more effective— much harder to ignore.

We chose four random but highly annoying sounds:

① Garbage Disposal "Errgrinerrrkk!"

② Mosquito Whine "Eeeeeeeeezzzz!"

Gonna eat ya!

③ Crying Baby "WAAAAAHHH!"

④ Slurping Soup "Schloop!"

I added pictures to try to make my presentation as fun as Carly's.

I thought it looked pretty good, I just hoped Sadie would do a decent job — and of course, Felix had to do his.

To make sure, I did something I'd never done before — I talked to Felix. I called his house the night before the science fair and he answered.

"Felix, it's Amelia," I said. "You know, one of your partners for the science fair project."

"What project? What science fair? What are you talking about?" He sounded panicked.

"The one everyone has to do if they don't want to fail science."

"I'm going to fail!" he squealed.

"No, you're not, because Sadie and I have done almost everything, but you're an essential part of the project so you <u>have</u> to go to the science fair tomorrow. We'll meet you at the gym at 9 a.m."

But I'm not prepared! I don't know what to do!

My dad will kill me! It's all over!

He was in high panic mode. We should have done an anxiety experiment instead of a sleep one.

I tried to calm him down. I promised him he wouldn't fail. All he had to do was be there — and be his usual self.

I'd always thought of Felix as a blobby, no-personality loser — it's hard to have a personality when you're asleep most of the time. But after talking to him, I felt sorry for him. Maybe there was a reason he always slept in class. Maybe he couldn't help it. Maybe he didn't want to be that way, but couldn't stay awake. I'd always assumed he was just lazy, but now I thought I was wrong. It wasn't that simple.

maybe he has a brother who snores even louder than Cleo or he lives above a bowling alley. ↓

Then I called Sadie to let her know Felix was meeting us tomorrow morning to set up everything.

"What if he doesn't sleep?" she asked.

"What?" I said.

"Science is before lunch, not first period. What if he doesn't fall asleep that early?"

"Don't worry — he'll fall asleep eventually and then we'll do the experiment." Even as I said it, I wondered if it was true. Why hadn't we thought of that before? Would ANYTHING go right with this project?

Saturday morning I got to Carly's house early and we walked to school together. I didn't want to show her my experiment description and I didn't want to see hers either. I just wanted to get the job done without any more worrying about messing up. Carly wasn't worried about that — she was nervous about whether her group would win a prize or not. That was something I didn't have to even think about.

The gym was already busy with kids setting up their projects.

"Wish me luck!" Carly said and she ran over to join Ezra and Letitia.

You don't need luck, I thought, you have a good group. I'm the one who needs luck — lots of it!

I saw Sadie in a back corner. She'd already grabbed a table for us and was putting together her part of the display. I had to admit, it didn't look bad. I guess I wasn't the only person in the group working hard (for once).

THE SCIENCE FAIR

COME TO LIGHT

I added my part to hers, and the whole thing looked → pretty good.

explanations, descriptions, ← conclusions

Ours and a bunch of bags of chips — was definitely the most appetizing display!

Everything looked okay except we were missing a vital part of the experiment — Felix.

"What will we do if he doesn't come?" Now it was Sadie's turn to be panicked. I expected mine to come next.

"Don't worry. He said he'd be here," I said.

"But what if he isn't?" she repeated.

Okay, now I was going to panic, too. She was right. He might not come, Or he could come, but not sleep. There was a heavy weight in my stomach. No matter how hard the two of us worked, our project was nothing without him, even though he hadn't done ANY work.

"You could pretend to be Felix," I suggested. "You know, act out his part. We could call it a simulation of the real thing." It was a lame idea, but better than nothing.

All around us kids were putting together their projects. A hum of talking filled the gym as parents, brothers, sisters, friends, and grandparents arrived. Lucky for me Cleo would much rather sleep late on a Saturday than come see the science fair. And Mom couldn't come, either. There was no one to see me fail except Sadie – and the whole 7th grade. And of course, the judges. When they walked in, the room got very quiet.
↓

↑
There was a wave machine.

↑
Something with prisms and beams of light

↑
model rockets

↑
a display on recycling that invited you to add to their bins

↑
a robot made from junk

The judges started at the front of the gym, so we had some time before they got to our table. I should have been really nervous and worried about Felix, but I wasn't. Instead I was excited about the other exhibits. After all, I couldn't control Felix any more than I could Sadie. I could only control myself, so I did what I wanted to do — I went over to Carly's project and watched her explain it to the judges. She was right — it was a lot of fun. And it was definitely the most interactive presentation there.

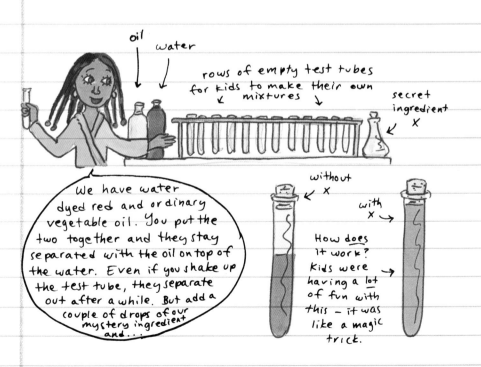

oil

water

rows of empty test tubes for kids to make their own mixtures

secret ingredient

X

We have water dyed red and ordinary vegetable oil. You put the two together and they stay separated with the oil on top of the water. Even if you shake up the test tube, they separate out after a while. But add a couple of drops of our mystery ingredient and...

without

X

with

X

How does it work? Kids were having a lot of fun with this — it was like a magic trick.

Carly started, then Letitia, and Ezra finished up. They really shared all the work.

So what is the mystery ingredient? Soap, ordinary dish soap! And how does it work? How does it allow oil and water to mix? It's simple — the soap molecules move between the oil and water molecules and bond with both.

It's like girl A hates girl C, but both like girl B, so when girl B is around, the three can be together, because B goes between A and C.

What a great explanation! And just as he said it, Felix showed up, our own mystery ingredient, the one who allowed Sadie and me to work together. He looked dazed and only half-awake (which was actually a good thing), but he was really there!

"Felix!" I waved to him. "Over here. We set up in the back."

"What am I supposed to do?" he asked.

"Nothing," I said, pulling up the chair I'd saved for him. "Pretend you're in science class. Just sit here and imagine Mr. Engels is talking."

He was asleep in two minutes! Sadie and I grinned at each other. We weren't friends, but we'd become good partners.

When the judges got to us, we explained our experiment, played our noises, and finished by opening up a bag of chips.

Felix looked up, startled.

bed head →

Is it time for lunch?

Everyone laughed, Sadie and me loudest of all. It wasn't great science, but it was fun, the kind of thing that belonged at a fair.

We didn't win a prize and neither did Carly's group — those went to exhibits on solar power, food additives, and how to build a better mouse-trap. I thought for sure Carly would be disappointed but she wasn't.

The winners were all really good science. Ours was more fun than scientific, but I think we did a good job. And so did you. Your project turned out great! I love the potato chip bags!

I nodded. "You know what? Despite all the problems, this was my best group project yet. I was so jealous of the kids in your group, but mine turned out just fine."

I waved good-bye to Sadie. She wasn't a friend, but she wasn't an enemy, either. She was the girl who asked a million questions. And Felix was the kid who was always asleep — luckily for us. He was snoring in the chair again — at least until someone opened up another bag of chips.

There was no cotton candy, no fried dough on a stick or silly prizes, but it had been a good science fair anyway. I felt like I'd been on a long, loopy roller coaster ride that was finally over.

Carly and I walked home together. She talked about what projects she should do next year. I told her I can't plan that yet. It all depends on who's in my group and what their special talents are. You never know!